1900; OR, THE LAST PRESIDENT

1900; OR, THE LAST PRESIDENT

BY

INGERSOLL LOCKWOOD

Aiwass Books
2019

1900; Or, The Last President by Ingersoll Lockwood. First published in 1896.

2019 edition published by Aiwass Books.

FIRST PRINTING 2019.

ISBN: 978-0-359-38437-2.

CONTENTS

"The Chicago Platform assumes, in fact, the form of a revolutionary propaganda. It embodies a menace of national disintegration and destruction."

- *Garret A. Hobart*

CHAPTER I

THAT WAS A TERRIBLE NIGHT for the great City of New York the night of Tuesday, November 3rd, 1896. The city staggered under the blow like a huge ocean liner which plunges, full speed, with terrific crash into a mighty iceberg, and recoils shattered and trembling like an aspen.

The people were gathered, lighthearted and confident, at the evening meal, when the news burst upon them. It was like a thunder bolt out of an azure sky: "Altgeld holds Illinois hard and fast in the Democratic line. This elects Bryan President of the United States!"

Strange to say, the people in the upper portion of the city made no movement to rush out of their houses and collect in the public squares, although the night was clear and beautiful. They sat as if paralyzed with a nameless dread, and when they conversed it was with bated breath and throbbing hearts. In less than half an hour, mounted policemen dashed through the streets calling out: "Keep within your houses; close your doors and barricade them. The entire East side is in a state of uproar. Mobs of vast size are organizing under the lead of Anarchists and Socialists, and threaten to plunder and despoil the houses of the rich who have wronged and oppressed them for so many years. Keep within doors. Extinguish all lights."

Happily, Governor Morton was in town, and although a deeper pallor overcame the ashen hue of age as he spoke, yet there was no tremor in his voice: "Let the Seventh, Twenty-second and Seventy-first regiments be ordered under arms." In a few moments hundreds of messengers could be heard racing through the silent streets, summoning the members of these regiments to their Armories.

Slowly, but with astonishing nerve and steadiness, the mobs pushed the police northward, and although the force stood the onslaught with magnificent courage, yet beaten back, the dark masses of infuriated beings surged up again with renewed fury and strength. "Will the troops be in time to save the city?" was the whispered inquiry among the knots of police officials who were directing the movements of their men.

About nine o'clock, with deafening outcries, the mob, like a four-headed monster breathing fire and flame, raced, tore, burst, raged into Union Square.

The police force was exhausted, but their front was still like a wall of stone, save that it was movable. The mob crowded it steadily to the north, while the air quivered and was rent with mad vociferations of the victors: "Bryan is elected! Bryan is elected! Our day has come at last. Down with our oppressors! Death to the rich man! Death to the goldbugs! Death to the capitalists! Give us back the money you have ground out of us. Give us back the marrow of our bones which you have used to grease the wheels of your chariots."

The police force was now almost helpless. The men still used their sticks, but the blows were ineffectual, and only served to increase the rage of the vast hordes now advancing upon Madison Square. The Fifth Avenue Hotel will be the first to feel the fury of the mob. Would the troops be in time to save it?

A half cheer, a half cry of joy goes up. It is inarticulate. Men draw a long breath; women drop upon their knees and strain their eyes; they can hear something, but they cannot see as yet, for the gashouses and electric plants had been destroyed by the mob early in the evening. They preferred to fight in the dark, or by the flames of rich men's abodes.

Again, a cheer goes up, louder and clearer this time, followed by cries of, "They're coming, they're coming."

Yes, they were coming; the Twenty-second down Broadway, the Seventh down Madison avenue, both on the double quick.

In a moment or so there were a few bugle calls, and a few spoken commands rang out clear and sharp; and then the two regiments stretched across the entire square, literally from wall to wall, in line of battle. The mob was upon them. Would this slender line of troops, could it hold such a mighty mass of men in check?

The answer was a deafening discharge of firearms, a terrific crack, such as some thunderbolts make when they explode. A wall of fire blazed across the Square. Again and again it blazed forth. The mob halted, stood fast, wavered, fell back, advanced again. At that moment there came a rattle as of huge knives in the distance. It was the gallant Seventy-first charging up Twenty-third street, and taking the mob on the flank. They came on like a wall of iron, bristling with blades of steel.

There were no outcries, no cheers from the regiment. It dealt out death in silence, save when two bayonets crossed and clashed in bearing down some doubly-vigorous foe.

As the bells rang out midnight, the last remnants of the mob were driven to cover, but the wheels of the dead wagons rattled till daybreak.

And then the aged Governor, in response to the Mayor's "Thank God, we've saved the city!" made answer: "Aye, but the Republic."

CHAPTER II

GREAT AS HAS BEEN the world's wonder at the uprising of Mr. Bryan's struggling masses "in the city by the sea," and the narrow escape of its magnificent homes from fire and brand, yet greater still was the wonderment when the news was flashed across the land that Chicago did not stand in need of a single Federal soldier.

"Chicago is mad, but it is the madness of joy. Chicago is in the hands of a mob, but it is a mob made up of her own people; noisy, rude and boisterous, the natural exultation of a suddenly enfranchised class; but bent on no other mischief than glorying over the villainous and self-seeking souls who have ground the faces of the poor and turned the pitiless screw of social and political power into the hearts of the 'common people' until its last thread had been reached, and despair pressed its lupine visage hard against the door of the laboring man."

And yet, at this moment when the night air quivered with the mad vociferations of the "common people," that the Lord had been good to them; that the wicked money-changers had been driven from the temple, that the stony-hearted usurers were beaten at last, that the "People's William" was at the helm now, that peace and plenty would in a few moons come back to the poor man's cottage, that Silver was King, aye. King at last, the world still went wondering why red-eyed anarchy, as she stood in Haymarket Square, with thin arms aloft, with wild mien and wilder gesticulation, drew no bomb of dynamite from her bosom, to hurl at the hated minions of the law who were silent spectators of this delirium of popular joy.

Why was it thus? Look and you shall know why white robed peace kept step with this turbulent band and turned its thought from red handed pillage. He was there. The master spirit to hold them in leash. He, and he alone, had lifted Bryan to his great eminence. Without these twenty-four electoral votes, Bryan had been doomed, hopelessly doomed. He, and he alone, held the great Commonwealth of the West hard and fast in the Democratic line; hence he came as conqueror, as King-maker, and the very walls of the sky-touching edifices trembled as he was dragged through the crowded streets by this orderly mob, and ten times ten thousand of his creatures bellowed his name and shook their hats aloft in mad exultation:

"You're our Savior, you've cleaned the Temple of Liberty of its foul horde of usurers. We salute you. We call you King-maker. Bryan shall call you Master too. You shall have your reward. You shall stand behind the throne. Your wisdom shall make us whole. You shall purge the land of this unlawful crowd of money lenders. You shall save the Republic. You are greater than Washington. You're a better friend of ours than Lincoln. You'll do more for us than Grant. We're your slaves. We salute you. We thank you. We bless you. Hurrah! Hurrah! Hurrah!"

But yet this vast throng of tamed monsters, this mighty mob of momentarily good-natured haters of established order, broke away from the master's control for a few brief moments, and dipped their hands in the enemy's blood.

The deed was swift as it was terrible. There were but four of them, unarmed, on pleasure bent. At sight of these men, a thousand throats belched out a deep and awful growl of hatred.

They were brave men, and backed against the wall to die like brave men, stricken down, beaten, torn, trampled, dragged, it was quick work. They had faced howling savages in the far West, painted monsters in human form, but never had they heard such yells leave the throats of men; and so they died, four brave men, clad in the blue livery of the Republic, whose only crime was that some months back, against the solemn protest of the Master, their comrades had set foot on the soil of the commonwealth, and saved the Metropolis of the West from the hands of this same mob.

And so Chicago celebrated the election of the new President who was to free the land from the grasp of the money-lenders, and undo the bad business of years of unholy union between barterers and sellers of human toil and the law makers of the land.

Throughout the length and breadth of the South, and beyond the Great Divide, the news struck hamlet and village like the glad tidings of a new evangel, almost as potent for human happiness as the heavenly message of two thousand years ago.

Bells rang out in joyful acclaim, and the very stars trembled at the telling, and the telling over and over of what had been done for the poor man by his brethren of the North, and around the blazing pine knots of the Southern cabin and in front of the mining camp fires of the Far West, the cry went up: "Silver is King! Silver is King!"

Black palms and white were clasped in this strange love-feast, and the dark-skinned grandchild no longer felt the sting of the lash on his sire's shoulder. All was peace and goodwill, for the people were at last victorious over their enemies who had taxed and tithed them into a very living death.

Now the laborer would not only be worthy of his hire, but it would be paid to him in a people's dollar, for the people's good, and now the rich man's coffers would be made to yield up their ill-gotten gain, and the sun would look upon this broad and fair land, and find no man without a market for the product of his labors. Henceforth, the rich man should, as was right and proper, pay a royal sum for the privilege of his happiness, and take the nation's taxes on his broad shoulders, where they belong.

CHAPTER III

THE PENS OF MANY WRITERS would not suffice to describe with anything like historical fullness and precision, the wild scenes of excitement which, on the morning after election day, burst forth on the floors of the various exchanges throughout the Union. The larger and more important the money center, the deeper, blacker and heavier the despair which sank upon them after the violent ebullitions of protest, defiance and execration had subsided.

With some, it seemed that visions of their swift but sure impoverishment only served to transform the dark and dismal drama of revolution and disintegration into a side-splitting farce, and they greeted the prospective loss of their millions with loud guffaws and indescribable antics of horseplay and unseemly mirth.

As the day wore on, the news became worse and worse. It was only too apparent that the House of Representatives of the Fifty-fifth Congress would be controlled by the combined vote of the Populists and Free Silver men, while the wild joy with which the entire South welcomed the election of Bryan and Sewall left little doubt in the minds of the Northern people that the Southern Senators would, to a man, range themselves on the Administration side of the great conflict into which the Republic was soon to be precipitated.

Add to these the twenty Senators of the Free Silver States of the North, and the new President would have the Congress of the Republic at his back. There would be nothing to stand between him and the realization of those schemes which an exuberant fancy, untamed by the hand of experience, and scornful of the leading strings of wisdom, can conjure up.

Did we say nothing? Nay, not so; for the Supreme Court was still there. And yet Justice Field had come fully up to the eightieth milestone in the journey of life and Justice Gray was nearly seventy, while one or two other members of this High Court of Judicature held to their lives with feeble grasp. Even in due and orderly course of events, why might there not come vacancies and then? In spite of the nameless dread that rested upon so many of our people, and chilled the very blood of the country's industries, the new year came hopefully, serenely, almost defiantly in.

There was an indescribable something in the air, a spirit of political devil-me-care, a feeling that the old order had passed away and that the Republic had entered into the womb of Time and been born again. This sentiment began to give outward and visible signs of its existence and growth in the remote agricultural districts of the South and Far West. They threw aside their working implements, loitered about, gathered in groups and the words Washington, White House, Silver, Bryan, Offices, Two for One, the South's Day, Reign of the Common People, Taxes, Incomes, Year of Jubilee, Free Coinage, Wall Street, Altgeld, Tillman, Peffer, Coxey, were whispered in a mysterious way with head noddings and pursing up of mouths.

As January wore away and February, slipping by, brought Bryan's Inauguration nearer and nearer, the groups melted into groups, and it was only too apparent that from a dozen different points in the South and North West "Coxey Armies" were forming for an advance on Washington. In some instances they were well clad and well provisioned; in others, they were little better than great bands of hungry and restless men, demoralized by idleness and wrought up to a strange degree of mental excitement by the extravagant harangues of their leaders, who were animated with but one thought, namely, to make use of these vast crowds of Silver Pilgrims, as they called themselves, to back up their claims for public office.

These crowds of deluded people were well named "Silver Pilgrims," for hundreds of them carried in hempen bags, pieces of silverware, in ninety-nine cases of a hundred. plated stuff of little value, which unscrupulous dealers and peddlers had palmed off upon them as sterling, with the promises that once in Washington, the United States Mint would coin their metal into "Bryan Dollars" giving "two for one" in payment for it.

While these motley "armies" marched upon the capitol of the Republic, the railway trains night and day brought vast crowds of "new men," politicians of low degree, men out of employment, drunken and disgruntled mechanics, farmer's sons, to seek their fortunes under the Reign of the People, heelers and hangers-on of ward bosses, old men who had not tasted office for thirty years and more, all inspired by Mr. Bryan's declaration that "The American people are not in favor of life tenure in the Civil Service, that a permanent office holding class is not in harmony with our institutions, that a fixed term in appointive offices would open the public service to a larger number of citizens, without impairing its efficiency," all bearing new besoms in their hands or across their shoulders, each and every one of them supremely confident that in the distribution of the spoils something would surely fall to his share, since they were the "Common People" who were so dear to Mr. Bryan, and who had made him President in the very face of the prodigious opposition of the rich men, whose coffers had been thrown wide open all to no purpose, and in spite too of the satanic and truly devilish power of that hell upon earth known as Wall Street, which had sweated gold in vain in its desperate efforts to fasten the chains of trusts and the claws of soulless monsters known as corporations upon these very "Common People," soon to march in triumph before the silver chariot of the young Conqueror from the West.

Chapter IV

There had been a strange prophecy put forth by someone, and it had made its way into the daily journals, and had been laughingly or seriously commented upon, according to the political tone of the paper, or the passing humor of the writer, that the 4th of March, 1897, would never dawn upon the American people.

There was something very curious and uncanny about the prediction, and what actually happened was not qualified to loosen the fearful tension of public anxiety, for the day literally and truly never dawned upon the City of Washington, and well deserves its historical name, the "Dawnless Day." At six o'clock, the hour of daybreak, such an impenetrable pall of clouds overhung the city that there came no signs of day.

The gathering crowds could plainly hear the plaintive cries and lamentations put up in the negro quarters of the city. Not until nearly nine o'clock did the light cease to "shine in darkness" and the darkness begin to comprehend it.

But although it was a cheerless gray day, even at high noon, its heaviness set no weight upon the spirits of the jubilant tens of thousands which completely filled the city and its public parks, and ran over into camps and hastily improvised shelters outside the city limits.

Not until the day previous had the President announced the names of those selected for his Cabinet.

The South and Far West were fairly beside themselves with joy, for there had been from their standpoint ugly rumors abroad for several days.

It had even been hinted that Bryan had surrendered to the "money changers," and that the selection of his constitutional advisers would prove him recreant to the glorious cause of popular government, and that the Reign of the Common People would remain but a dream of the "struggling masses."

But these apprehensions were short lived. The young President stood firm and fast on the platform of the parties which had raised him to his proud eminence.

And what better proof of his thorough belief in himself and in his mission could he have given than the following: Secretary of State—William M. Stewart, of Nevada. Secretary of Treasury—Richard P. Bland, of Missouri. Secretary of War—John P. Altgeld, of Illinois. Attorney General—Roger Q. Mills, of Texas. Postmaster General—Henry George, of New York. Secretary Navy— John Gary Evans, of South Carolina. Secretary Interior— William A. Peffer, of Kansas. Secretary Agriculture—Lafe Pence, of Colorado.

The first thing that flashed across the minds of many upon glancing over this list of names was the omission therefrom of Tillman's. What did it mean? Could the young President have quarreled with his best friend, his most powerful coadjutor?

But the wiser ones only shook their heads and made answer that it was Tillman's hand that filled the blank for Secretary of the Navy, left there by the new ruler after the people's own heart.

Evans was but a creation of this great Commoner of the South, an image graven with his hands.

The inaugural address was not a disappointment to those who had come to hear it. It was like the man who delivered it: bold, outspoken, unmistakable in its terms, promising much, impatient of precedent, reckless of result; a double confirmation that this was to be the Reign of the Common People, that much should be unmade and much made over, and no matter how the rich man might cry out in anger or amazement, the nation must march on to the fulfillment of a higher and nobler mission than the impoverishment and degradation of the millions for the enrichment and elevation of the few.

Scarcely had the young President—his large eyes filled with a strange light, and his smooth, hairless visage radiant as a cloudless sky, his wife's arm twined around his, and their hands linked in those of their children— passed within the lofty portal of the White House, then he threw himself into a chair, and seizing a sheet of official paper penned the following order, and directed its immediate promulgation:

EXECUTIVE MANSION, WASHINGTON, D.C.
MARCH 4TH, 1897.

EXECUTIVE ORDER No. 1.

IN ORDER THAT THERE MAY BE IMMEDIATE RELIEF IN THE TERRIBLE FINANCIAL DEPRESSION NOW WEIGHING UPON OUR BELOVED COUNTRY, CONSEQUENT UPON AND RESULTING FROM THE UNLAWFUL COMBINATION OF CAPITALISTS AND MONEY-LENDERS BOTH IN THIS REPUBLIC AND IN ENGLAND, AND THAT THE RUINOUS AND INEVITABLE PROGRESS TOWARD A UNIVERSAL GOLD STANDARD MAY BE STAYED, THE PRESIDENT ORDERS AND DIRECTS THE IMMEDIATE ABANDONMENT OF THE SO-CALLED "GOLD RESERVE," AND THAT ON AND AFTER THE PROMULGATION OF THIS ORDER, THE GOLD AND SILVER STANDARD OF THE CONSTITUTION BE RESUMED AND STRICTLY MAINTAINED IN ALL THE BUSINESS TRANSACTIONS OF THE GOVERNMENT.

It was two o'clock in the afternoon when news of this now world-famous Executive Order was flashed into the great banking centers of the country. Its effect on Wall street beggars description.

On the floor of the Stock Exchange men yelled and shrieked like painted savages, and, in their mad struggles, tore and trampled each other. Many dropped in fainting fits, or fell exhausted from their wild and senseless efforts to say what none would listen to. Ashen pallor crept over the faces of some, while the blood threatened to burst the swollen arteries that spread in purple network over the brows of others.

When silence came at last, it was a silence broken by sobs and groans. Some wept, while others stood dumbstricken as if it was all a bad dream, and they were awaiting the return of their poor distraught senses to set them right again.

Ambulances were hastily summoned and fainting and exhausted forms were borne through hushed and whispering masses wedged into Wall street, to be whirled away uptown to their residences, there to come into full possession of their senses only to cry out in their anguish that ruin, black ruin, stared them in the face if this news from Washington should prove true.

CHAPTER V

BY PROCLAMATION BEARING DATE the 5th day of March 1897, the President summoned both houses of Congress to convene in extraordinary session "for the consideration of the general welfare of the United States, and to take such action as might seem necessary and expedient to them on certain measures which he should recommend to their consideration, measures of vital import to the welfare and happiness of the people, if not to the very existence of the Union and the continuance of their enjoyment of the liberties achieved by the fathers of the Republic."

While awaiting the day set for the coming together of the Congress, the "Great Friend of the Common People" came suddenly face to face with the first serious business of his Administration. Fifty thousand people tramped the streets of Washington without bread or shelter.

Many had come in quest of office, lured on by the solemn pronouncement of their candidate that there should be at once a clean sweep of these barnacles of the ship of State and so complete had been their confidence in their glorious young captain, that they had literally failed to provide themselves with either "purse or script or shoes," and now stood hungry and footsore at his gate, begging for a crust of bread.

But most of those making up this vast multitude were "the unarmed warriors of peaceful armies" like the one once led by the redoubtable Coxey, decoyed from farm and hamlet and plantation by some nameless longing to "go forth" to stand in the presence of this new

Savior of Society, whose advent to power was to bring them "double pay" for all their toil.

While on the march all had gone well, for their brethren had opened their hearts and their houses as these "unarmed warriors" had marched with flying banners and loud huzzas through the various towns on the route.

But now the holiday was over, they were far from their homes, they were in danger of perishing from hunger. What was to be done "They are our people," said the President, "their love of country has undone them; the nation must not let them suffer, for they are its hope and its shield in the hour of war, and its glory and its refuge in times of peace. They are the common people for whose benefit this Republic was established. The Kings of the earth may desert them; I never shall."

The Secretary of War was directed to establish camps in the parks and suburbs of the city and to issue rations and blankets to these luckless wanderers until the Government could provide for their transportation back to their homes. On Monday, March 15th, the President received the usual notification from both houses of Congress, that they had organized and were ready for the consideration of such measures as he might choose to recommend for their action.

The first act to pass both houses and receive the signature of the President, was an Act repealing the Act of 1873, and opening the mints of the United States to the free coinage of silver at the ratio of sixteen to one, with gold, and establishing branch mints in the cities of Denver, Omaha, Chicago, Kansas City, Spokane, Los Angeles, Charleston and Mobile.

The announcement that reparation had thus been made to the people for the "Crime of 1873" was received with loud cheering on the floors and in the galleries of both houses.

And the Great North heard these cheers and trembled.

The next measure of great public import brought before the House was an act to provide additional revenue by levying a tax upon the incomes, substantially on the lines laid down by the legislation of 1894.

The Republican Senators strove to make some show of resistance to this measure, but so solid were the administration ranks, that they only succeeded in delaying it for a few weeks. This first skirmish with the enemy, however, brought the President and his followers to a realizing sense that not only must the Senate be shorn of its power to block the "new movement of regeneration and reform" by the adoption of rules cutting off prolonged debate, but that the "new dispensation" must at once proceed to increase its senatorial representation, for who could tell what moment some one of the Northern Silver States might not slip away from its allegiance to the "Friend of the Common People."

The introduction of a bill repealing the various Civil Service acts passed for the alleged purpose of "regulating and improving the Civil Service of the United States," and of another repealing the various acts establishing National Banks, and substituting United States notes for all national bank notes based upon interest bearing bonds, opened the eyes of the Republican opposition to the fact that the President and his party were possessed of the courage of their convictions, and were determined, come good report or evil report, to wipe all conflicting legislation from the statute books.

The battle in the Senate now took on a spirit of extreme acrimony; scenes not witnessed since the days of Slavery, were of daily occurrence on the floors of both the House and the Senate. Threats of secession came openly from the North only to be met with the jeers and laughter of the silver and populist members. "We're in the saddle at last," exclaimed a Southern member, "and we intend to ride on to victory!"

The introduction of bills for the admission of New Mexico and Arizona, and for the division of Texas into two States to be called East Texas and West Texas, although each of these measures was strictly within the letter of the Constitution, fell among the members of the Republican opposition like a torch in a house of tinder. There was fire at once, and the blaze of party spirit leapt to such dangerous heights that the whole nation looked on in consternation.

Was the Union about to go up in a great conflagration and leave behind it but the ashes and charred pedestals of its greatness?

"We are the people," wrote the President in lines of dignity and calmness. "We are the people and what we do, we do under the holy sanction of law, and there is no one so powerful or so bold as to dare to say we do not do well in lifting off the nation's shoulders the grievous and unlawful burdens which preceding Congresses have placed upon them."

And so the "Long Session" of the fifty-fifth Congress was entered upon, fated to last through summer heat and autumn chill, and until winter came again and the Constitution itself set limits to its lasting.

And when that day came, and its speaker, amid a wild tumult of cheers, arose to declare it ended not by their will, but by the law of the land, he said: "The glorious revolution is in its brightest bud. Since the President called upon us to convene in last March, we have with the strong blade of public indignation, and with a full sense of our responsibility, erased from the statute books the marks of our country's shame and our people's subjugation. Liberty can not die.

"There remains much to be done in the way of building up. Let us take heart and push on. On Monday, the regular session of this Congress will begin. We must greet our loved ones from the distance. We have no time to go home and embrace them."

CHAPTER VI

WHEN A REPUBLICAN MEMBER of the House arose to
move the usual adjournment for the holidays, there was
a storm of hisses and cries of "No, no!" said the leader of
the House, amid deafening plaudits: "We are the servants
of the people. Our work is not yet complete. There must
be no play for us while coal barons stand with their feet
on the ashes of the poor man's hearthstone, and weeds
and thorns cumber the fields of the farmer for lack of
money to buy seed and implements. There must be no
play for us while railway magnates press from the pockets of the laboring man six and eight per cent return on
thrice watered stocks, and rapacious landlords, enriched
by inheritance, grind the faces of the poor.

"There must be no play for us while enemies of the
human kind are, by means of trust and combination and
'corners,' engaged in drawing their unholy millions from
the very lifeblood of the nation, paralyzing its best efforts
and setting the blight of intemperance and indifference
upon it, by making life but one long struggle for existence, without a gleam of rest and comfort in old age. No,
Mr. Speaker, we must not adjourn, but by our efforts in
these halls of legislation let the nation know that we are
at work for its emancipation, and by these means let the
monopolists and money-changers be brought to a realizing sense that the Reign of the Common People has really
been entered upon, and then the bells will ring out a
happier, gladder New Year than has ever dawned upon
this Republic."

The opposition fairly quailed before the vigor and ear-
nestness of the "new dispensation."

There were soon before the House and pressed well on toward final passage a number of important measures calculated to awaken an intense feeling of enthusiasm among the working classes.

Among these was an Act establishing a Loan Commission for the loaning of certain moneys of the United States to Farmers and Planters without interest; an Act for the establishment of a permanent Department of Public Works, its head to be styled Secretary of Public Works, rank as a cabinet officer, and supervise the expenditure of all public moneys for the construction of public buildings and the improvement of rivers and harbors; an Act making it a felony, punishable with imprisonment for life, for any citizen or combination of citizens to enter into any trust or agreement to stifle, suppress or in any way interfere with full, open and fair competition in trade and manufacture among the States, or to make use of any interstate railroads, waterways or canals for the transportation of any food products or goods, wares or merchandise which may have been "cornered," stored or withheld with a view to enhance the value thereof.

And, most important of all, a preliminary Act having for its object the appointment of Commissioners for the purchase by the Federal Government of all interstate railway and telegraph lines, and in the meantime the strict regulation of all fares and charges by a Government Commission, from whose established schedules there shall be no appeal. On Washington's Birthday the President issued an Address of Congratulation to the People of the United States, from which the following is extracted:

"The malicious prognostications of our political opponents have proven themselves to be but empty sound and fury.

"Although not quite one year has elapsed since I, agreeable to your mandate, restored to you the money of the Constitution, yet from every section of our Union comes the glad tidings of renewed activity and prosperity. The working man no longer sits cold and hungry beside a cheerless hearthstone; the farmer has taken heart and resumed work; the wheels of the factory are in motion again; the shops and stores of the legitimate dealer and trader are full of bustle and action. There is content everywhere, save in the counting-room of the money-changer, for which thank God and the common people of this Republic.

"The free coinage of that metal which the Creator, in His wisdom, stored with so lavish a hand in the subterranean vaults of our glorious mountain ranges, has proven a rich and manifold blessing for our people. It is in every sense of the word the 'people's money,' and already the envious world looks on in amazement that we have shown our ability to do without 'foreign cooperation.' The Congress of our Republic has been in almost continuous session since I took my oath of office, and the administration members deserve your deepest and most heartfelt gratitude. They are rearing for themselves a monument more lasting than chiseled bronze or polished monolith. They knew no rest, they asked for no respite from their labors until, at my earnest request, they adjourned over to join their fellow citizens in the observance of this sacred anniversary.

"Fellow citizens, remember the bonds which a wicked and selfish class of usurers and speculators fastened upon you, and on this anniversary of the birth of the Father of our Country, let us renew our pledges to undo completely and absolutely their infamous work, and in public assembly and family circle, let us by new vows confirm our love of right and justice, so that the great gain may not slip away from us, but go on increasing so long as the statute books contain a single trace of the record of our enslavement. As for me, I have but one ambition, and that is to deserve so well of you that when you come to write my epitaph, you set beneath my name the single line: "Here lies a Friend of the Common People."

CHAPTER VII

THIS FIRST YEAR OF THE Silver Administration was scarcely rounded up, ere there began to be ugly rumors that the Government was no longer able to hold the white metal at a parity with gold. "It is the work of Wall Street," cried the friends of the President, but wiser heads were shaken in contradiction, for they had watched the sowing of the wind of unreason, and knew only too well that the whirlwind of folly must be reaped in due season.

The country had been literally submerged by a silver flood which had poured its argent waves into every nook and cranny of the Republic, stimulating human endeavor to most unnatural and harmful vigor. Mad speculation stalked over the land. People sold what they should have clung to, and bought what they did not need. Manufacturers heaped up goods for which there was no demand, and farmers ploughed where they had not drained and drained, where they were never fated to plough.

The small dealer enlarged his business with more haste than judgment, and the widow drew her mite from the bank of savings to buy land on which she was destined never to set foot. The spirit of greed and gain lodged in every mind, and the "Common People" with a mad eagerness loosened the strings of their leather purses to cast their hard earned savings into wild schemes of profit. Every scrap and bit of the white metal that they could lay their hands upon, spoons hallowed by the touch of lips long since closed in death, and cups and tankards from which grand sires had drunken were bundled away to the mints to be coined into "people's dollars."

At the very first rumor of the slipping away of this trusted coin from its parity with gold, there was a fearful awakening, like the start and the gasp of the miser who sees his horded treasure melting away from before his eyes, and he not able to reach out and stay its going. Protest and expostulation first, then came groans and prayers, from which there was an easy road to curses. The working man threw off his cap and apron to rush upon the public square, and demand his rights. Mobs ran together, processions formed, deputations hurried off to Washington, not on foot like the Coxey Army, but on the swift wings of the Limited Express.

The "common people" were admitted to the bar of the house, their plaints patiently listened to, and reparation promised. Bills for increased revenue were hurriedly introduced, and new taxes were loaded upon the broad shoulders of the millionaires of the nation; taxes on checks, taxes on certificates of incorporation, taxes on deeds and mortgages, taxes on pleasure yachts, taxes on private parks and *plaisances*, taxes on wills of all property above $5,000 in value, taxes on all gifts of realty for and in consideration of natural love and affection, taxes on all passage tickets to foreign lands, and double taxes on the estates of all absentees on and after the lapse of six months.

There was a doubling up too of the tariff on all important luxuries, for as was said on the floor of Congress, "if the silks and satins of American looms and the wines and tobacco of native growth, are not good enough for 'my Lord of Wall Street,' let him pay the difference and thank heaven that he can get them at that price."

To quiet the murmurs of the good people of the land, additional millions were placed to the credit of the Department of Public Works, and harbors were dredged out in one month only to fill up in the next, and new systems of improvement of interstate waterways were entered upon on a scale of magnitude hitherto undreamt of.

The Commissioners for the distribution of public moneys to farmers so impoverished as to be unable to work their lands, were kept busy in placing "Peffer Loans" where the need of them seemed to be the greatest, and to put a stop to the "nefarious doings" of money changers and traders in the misfortunes of the people, a statute was enacted making it a felony punishable with imprisonment for life, for any person or corporate body to buy and sell government bonds or public funds, or deal in them with a view to draw gain or profit from their rise and fall in value.

But try never so hard, the Government found itself powerless to check the slow but steady decline in value of the people's dollar. By midsummer, it had fallen to forty-three cents, and ere the fair Northland had wrapped itself, like a scornful beauty, in its Autumn mantle of gold, the fondly trusted coin had sunk to exactly one-third of the value of a standard gold dollar.

People carried baskets in their arms, filled with the now discredited coin, when they went abroad to pay a debt or make purchase of the necessaries of life. Hugh sacks of the white metal were flung at the door of the mortgagee when discharge was sought for a few thousand dollars.

Men servants accompanied their mistresses upon shopping tours to carry the necessary funds, and leather pockets took the place of the old time muslin ones in male habiliments, least the weight of the fifteen coins required to make up a five dollar gold piece should tear the thin stuff and spill a dollar at every step.

All day long in the large cities, huge trucks loaded with sacks of the coin rolled and rumbled over the pavement in the adjustment of the business balances of the day. The tradesman who called for his bill was met at the door with a coal scuttle or a nail keg filled with the needful amount, and on pay day, the working man took his eldest boy with him to "tote the stuff home" while he carried the usual bundle of firewood.

And strange to say, this dollar, once so beloved by the "common people," parted with its very nature of riches and lay in heaps unnoticed and unheeded on shelf or table, until occasion arose to pay it out which was done with a careless and contemptuous toss as if it were the iron money of the ancient Spartans, and Holy Writ for once at least, was disproven and discredited for the thief showed not the slightest inclination to "break in and steal" where these treasures had been laid up on earth, although the discs of white metal might lie in full view on the table, like so many pewter platters or pieces of tinware.

Men let debts run, rather than call for them, and barter and exchange came into vogue again, the good housewife calling on her neighbor for a loan of flour or meal, promising to return the same in sugar or dried fruit whenever the need might arise.

And still the once magic discs of silver slipped slowly and silently downward, and ever downward in value and good name, until it almost seemed as if the people hated the very name of silver.

CHAPTER VIII

THE "FATEFUL YEAR OF '99" upon its coming in, found the Republic of Washington in dire and dangerous straits. The commercial and industrial boom had spent its force, and now the frightful evils of a debased currency, coupled with demoralizing effects of rampant paternalism, were gradually strangling the land to death.

Capital, ever timid and distrustful in such times, hid itself in safe deposit vaults, or fled to Europe. Labor, although really hard pressed and lacking the very necessities of life, was loudmouthed and defiant. Socialism and Anarchism found willing ears into which to pour their burning words of hatred and malevolence, and the consequence was that serious rioting broke out in the larger cities of the North, often taxing the capacities of the local authorities to the utmost.

It was bruited abroad that violent dissensions had arisen in the Cabinet, the young President giving signs of a marked change of mind, and like many a man who has appealed to the darker passions of the human heart, he seemed almost ready to exclaim: "I stand alone. The spirits I have called up are no longer obedient to me. My country, oh, my country, how willingly would I give my life for thee, if by such a sacrifice I could restore thee to thy old time prosperity."

For the first he began to realize what an intense spirit of sectionalism had entered into this "revolutionary propaganda." He spoke of his fears to none save to his wise and prudent helpmate. "I trust you, beloved," she whispered, as she pressed the broad, strong hands that held her enclasped. "Ay, dear one, but does my country?" came in almost a groan from the lips of the youthful ruler. Most evident was it, that thus far the South had been the great gainer in this struggle for power.

She had increased her strength in the Senate by six votes; she had regained her old time prestige in the House; one of her most trusted sons was in the Speaker's chair, while another brilliant Southron led the administration forces on the floor. Born as she was for the brilliant exercise of intellectual vigor; the South was of that strain of blood which knows how to wear the kingly graces of power so as best to impress the "common people." Many of the men of the North had been charmed and fascinated by this natural pomp and inborn demeanor of greatness and had yielded to it.

Not a month had gone by that this now dominant section had not made some new demand upon the country at large. Early in the session, at its request, the internal revenue tax which had rested so long upon the tobacco crop of the South, and poured so many millions of revenue into the national treasury, was wiped from the statute books with but a feeble protest from the North.

But now the country was thrown into a state bordering upon frenzy by a new demand, which, although couched in calm and decorous terms, nay, almost in the guise of a petition for long-delayed justice to hard-pressed and suffering brethren, had about it a suppressed, yet unmistakable tone of conscious power and imperiousness which well became the leader who spoke for "that glorious Southland to which this Union owes so much of its greatness and its prestige."

Said he, "Mr. Speaker, for nearly thirty years our people, although left impoverished by the conflict of the states, have given of their substance to salve the wounds and make green the old age of the men who conquered us. We have paid this heavy tax, this fearful blood money unmurmuringly. You have forgiven us for our bold strike for liberty that God willed should not succeed. You have given us back our rights, opened the doors of these sacred halls to us, called us your brothers, but unlike noble Germany who was content to exact a lump sum from "la belle France," and then bid her go in peace and freedom from all further exactions, you have for nearly thirty years laid this humiliating war tax upon us, and thus forced us year in and year out to kiss the very hand that smote us.

"Are we human that we now cry out against it? Are we men that we feel nothing in our veins after these long years of punishment for no greater crime than that we loved liberty better than the bonds of a confederation laid upon us by our fathers? We appeal to you as our brothers and our countrymen. Lift this infamous tax from our land, than which your great North is ten thousand times richer. Do one of two things: Either take our aged and decrepit soldiers by the hand and bless their last days with pensions from the treasury of our common country, for they were only wrong in that their cause failed, or remove this hated tax and make such restitution of this blood money as shall seem just and equitable to your soberer and better judgment."

To say that this speech, of which the foregoing is but a brief extract, threw both Houses of Congress into most violent disorder, but faintly describes its effect. Cries of treason, treason! went up; blows were exchanged and hand to hand struggles took place in the galleries, followed by the flash of the dread bowie and the crack of the ready pistol. The Republic was shaken to its very foundations. Throughout the North there was but a repetition of the scenes that followed the firing upon Sumter.

Public meetings were held, and resolutions passed calling upon the Government to concentrate troops in and about Washington, and prepare for the suppression of a second Rebellion.

But gradually this outbreak of popular indignation lost some of its strength and virulence, for it was easy to comprehend that nothing would be gained at this stage of the matter by meeting a violent and unlawful demand with violence and unwise counsels.

Besides, what was it any way but the idle threat of a certain clique of unscrupulous politicians? The Republic stood upon too firm a foundation to be shaken by mere appeals to the passions of the hour. To commit treason against our country called for an overt act. What had it to dread from the mere oratorical flash of a passing storm of feeling?

It is hard to say what the young President thought of these scenes in Congress. So pale had he grown of late that a little more of pallor would pass unnoted, but those who were wont to look upon his face in these troublous times report that in the short space of a few days the lines in his countenance deepened perceptibly, and that a firmer and stronger expression of willpower lurked in the corners of his wide mouth, overhung his square and massive chin, and accentuated the vibrations of his wide-opened nostrils.

He was under a terrible strain. When he had caught up the scepter of power, it seemed a mere bauble in his strong grasp, but now it had grown strangely heavy, and there was a mysterious pricking at his brow, as if that crown of thorns which he had not willed should be set upon the heads of others, were being pressed down with cruel hands upon His own.

CHAPTER IX

WHEN THE LAST EMBERS of the great conflagration of the Rebellion had been smothered out with tears for the Lost Cause, a prophecy had gone up that the mighty North, rich with a hundred great cities, and strong in the conscious power of its wide empire, would be the next to raise the standard of rebellion against the Federal Government. But that prophet was without honor in his own land, and none had paid heed to his seemingly wild words.

Yet now, this same mighty North sat there in her grief and anxiety, with her face turned Southward, and her ear strained to catch the whispers that were in the air. Had not the scepter of power passed from her hand forever? Was not the Revolution complete? Were not the Populists and their allies firmly seated in the Halls of Congress?

Had not the Supreme Court been rendered powerless for good by packing it with the most uncompromising adherents of the new political faith? Had not the very nature of the Federal Government undergone a change: Was not Paternalism rampant? Was not Socialism on the increase? Were there not everywhere evidences of an intense hatred of the North and a firm determination to throw the whole burden of taxation upon the shoulders of the rich man, in order that the surplus revenues of the Government might be distributed among those who constitute the "common people?"

How could this section of the Union ever hope to make head against the South, united, as it now was, with the rapidly growing States of the Northwest?

Could the magnificent cities of the North content themselves to march at the tail of Tillman's and Peffer's chariots? Had not the South a firm hold of the Senate?

Where was there a ray of hope that the North could ever again regain its lost power, and could it for a single moment think of entrusting its vast interests to the hands of a people differing with them on every important question of statecraft, pledged to a policy that could not be otherwise than ruinous to the welfare of the grand commonwealths of the Middle and Eastern sections of the Union and their sister States this side of the Mississippi: It were madness to think of it.

The plunge must be taken, the declaration must be made. There was no other alternative, save abject submission to the chieftains of the new dispensation, and the complete transformation of that vast social and political system vaguely called the North.

But this revolution within a revolution would be a bloodless one, for there could be no thought of coercion, no serious notion of checking such a mighty movement. It would be in reality the true Republic purging itself of a dangerous malady, sloughing off a diseased and gangrened member; no more, no less.

Already this mighty movement of withdrawals from the Witenagemote of the Union was in the air. People spoke of it in a whisper, or with bated breath; but as they turned it over and over in their minds, it took on shape and form and force, till at last it burst into life and action like Minerva from Jupiter's brain: full-fledged, full-armed, full-voiced and full-hearted.

Really, why would it not be all for the best that this mighty empire, rapidly growing so vast and unwieldy as to be only with the greatest difficulty governable from a single center, should be split into three parts, Eastern, Southern and Western, now that it may be done without dangerous jar or friction? The three republics could be federated for purposes offensive and defensive, and until these great and radical changes could be brought about there would be no great difficulty in devising "living terms," for immediately upon the Declaration of Dissolution, each State would become repossessed of the sovereign powers which it had delegated to the Federal Government.

Meanwhile the "Fateful year '99" went onward toward its close. The whole land seemed stricken with paralysis, so far as the various industries were concerned, but, as it is wont to be in such times, men's minds were supernaturally active. The days were passed in the reading of public prints, or in passing in review the weighty events of the hour.

The North was only waiting for an opportunity to act. But the question that perplexed the wisest heads was: How and when shall the Declaration of Dissolution be made, and how soon thereafter shall the North and the States in sympathy with her withdraw from the Union, and declare to the world their intention to set up a republic of their own, with the mighty metropolis of New York as its social, political and commercial center and capital? As it came to pass, the North had not long to wait.

The Fifty-sixth Congress soon to convene in regular session in the city of Washington, was even more Populistic and Socialistic than its famous predecessor, which had wrought such wonderful changes in the law of the land, showing no respect for precedent, no reverence for the old order of things.

Hence all eyes were fixed upon the capital of the nation, all roads were untrodden, save those which led to Washington.

CHAPTER X

AGAIN CONGRESS HAD REFUSED to adjourn over for the holidays. The leaders of the Administration forces were unwilling to close their eyes, even for needful sleep, and went about pale and haggard, startled at every word and gesture of the opposition, like true conspirators, as they were, for the Federal troops had been almost to a man quietly removed from the Capital and its vicinage, lest the President in a moment of weakness, might do or suffer to be done some act unfriendly to the Reign of the Common People.

Strange as it may seem, there had been very little note taken by the country at large of the introduction at the opening of the session of an Act to extend the Pension System of the United States to the Soldiers of the Confederate Armies, and for covering back into the various treasuries of certain States of the Union, such portions of internal revenue taxes collected since the re-admission of said states to the Federal Congress, as may be determined by Commissioners duly appointed under said Act. Was it the calm of despair, the stolidity of desperation, or the cool and restrained energy of a noble and refined courage?

The introduction of the Act, however, had one effect; it set in motion toward the National capital, mighty streams of humanity, not of wild-eyed fanatics or unshaven and unkempt politicasters and bezonians, but of soberly-clad citizens with a business-like air about them, evidently men who knew how to earn more than enough for a living, men who paid their taxes and had a right to take a look at the public servants, if desire so moved them.

But very plain was it that the mightier stream flowed in from the South, and those who remembered the Capital in antebellum days, smiled at the old familiar sight, the clean-shaven faces, the long hair thrown carelessly tack under the broad brim felts, the half unbuttoned waistcoats and turn down collars, the small feet and neatly fitting boots, the springy loping pace, the soft negroese intonation, the long fragrant cheroot.

It was easy to pick out the man from the Northland, well-clad and well-groomed, as careful of his linen as a woman, prim and trim, disdainful of the picturesque felts, ever crowned with the ceremonious derby, the man of affairs, taking a business-like view of life, but wearing for the nonce a worried look and drawing ever and anon a deep breath.

The black man, ever at the heels of his white brother, set to rule over him by an inscrutable decree of nature, came forth too in thousands, chatting and laughing gayly, careless of the why or wherefore of his white brother's deep concern, and powerless to comprehend it had he so desired. Every hour now added to the throng. The broad avenues were none too broad.

The excitement increased. Men talked louder and louder, women and children disappeared almost completely from the streets. The "Southern element" drew more and more apart in knots and groups by itself. Men threw themselves upon their beds to catch a few hours' sleep, but without undressing, as if they were expecting the happening of some portentous event at any moment, the event of their lives, and dreaded the thought of being a moment late.

If all went well, the bill would come up for final passage on Saturday, the 30th day of the month, but so fierce was the battle raged against it, and so frequent the interruptions by the contumacy both of members and of the various cliques crowding the galleries to suffocation, that little or no progress could be made. The leaders of the administration forces saw midnight drawing near with no prospect of attaining their object before the coming in of Sunday on which the House had never been known to sit. An adjournment over to Monday of the New Year might be fatal, for who could tell what unforeseen force might not break up their solid ranks and throw them into confusion. They must rise equal to the occasion.

A motion was made to suspend the rules, and to remain in continuous session until the business before the House was completed. Cries of "Unprecedented!" "Revolutionary!" "Monstrous!" came from the opposition, but all to no purpose; the House settled down to its work with such a grim determination to conquer that the Republican minority fairly quailed before it.

Food and drink were brought to the members in their seats; they ate, drank and slept at their posts, like soldiers determined not to be ambushed or stampeded. It was a strange sight, and yet an impressive one withal; a great party struggling for long deferred rights, freemen jealous of their liberties, bound together with the steel hooks of determination that only death might break asunder. of Sunday came in at last, and still the struggle went on.

"The people know no days when their liberties are at stake," cried the leader of the House. "The Sabbath was made for man and not man for the Sabbath."

Many of the speeches delivered on that famous Sunday sounded more like the lamentations of a Jeremiah, the earnest and burning utterances of a Paul, or the scholarly and well-rounded periods of an Apollos.

The weary hours were lightened by the singing of hymns by the Southern members, most of them good

Methodists, in which their friends and sympathizers in the galleries joined full throated and fuller hearted; while at times, clear, resonant and in perfect unison, the voices of the staunch men of the North broke in and drowned out the religious song with the majestic and soul-stirring measures of "John Brown's Body," the "Glory, Glory Halleluiah" of which seemed to hush the tumult of the Chamber like a weird chant of some invisible chorus breaking in upon the fierce rioting of a Belshazzar's feast.

Somewhat after eleven o'clock, an ominous silence sank upon the opposing camps, the Republican leaders could be seen conferring together nervously. It was a sacred hour of night, thrice sacred for the great Republic. Not only a New Year, but a New Century was about to break upon the world. A strange hush crept over the turbulent House, and its still more turbulent galleries.

The Republican leader rose to his feet. His voice sounded cold and hollow. Strong men shivered as they listened.

"Mr. Speaker: We have done our duty to our country; we have nothing more to say, no more blows to strike. We cannot stand here within the sacred precincts of this Chamber, and see our rights as freemen trampled beneath the feet of the majority. We have striven to prevent the downfall of the Republic, like men sworn to battle against wrong and tyranny, but there comes a time when blank despair seizes upon the hearts of those who struggle against overwhelming odds.

"That hour has sounded for us We believe our people, the great and generous people of the North, will cry unto us: Well done, good and faithful servants. If we do wrong, let them condemn us. We, every man of us, Mr. Speaker, have but this moment sworn not to stand within this Chamber and witness the passage of this act. Therefore we go …"

"Not so, my countrymen," cried a clear metallic far-reaching voice that sounded through the Chamber with an almost supernatural ring in it. In an instant, every head was turned and a thousand voices burst out with suppressed force: "The President! The President!"

In truth, it was he, standing at the bar of the House, wearing the visage of death rather than of life. The next instant the House and galleries burst into a deafening clamor which rolled up and back in mighty waves that shook the very walls. There was no stilling it. Again and again it burst forth, the mingling of ten thousand words, howling, rumbling and groaning like the warring elements of nature.

Several times the President stretched forth his great white hands appealing for silence, while the dew of mingled dread and anguish beaded on his brow and trickled down his cheeks in liquid supplication that his people might either slay him or listen to him. The tumult stilled its fury for a moment, and he could be heard saying brokenly: "My countrymen, oh, my countrymen ..."

But the quick sharp sound of the gavel cut him short.

"The President must withdraw," said the Speaker, calmly and coldly, "his presence here is a menace to our free deliberation."

Again the tumult set up its deafening roar, while a look of almost horror overspread the countenance of the Chief Magistrate. Once more his great white hands went heavenward, pleading for silence with such a mute majesty of supplication, that silence fell upon the immense assemblage, and his lips moved not in vain.

"Gentlemen of the House of Representatives, I stand here upon my just and lawful right as President of the Republic, to give you 'information of the state of the Union.' I have summoned the Honorable the Senate, to meet me in this Chamber.

"I call upon you to calm your passions, and give ear to me as your oath of office sets the sacred obligation upon you."

There was a tone of godlike authority in these few words, almost divine enough to make the winds obey and still the tempestuous sea. In deepest silence, and with a certain show of rude and native grandeur of bearing, the Senators made their entrance into the Chamber, the members of the House rising, and the Speaker advancing to meet the Vice President.

The spectacle was grand and moving. Tears gathered in eyes long unused to them, and at an almost imperceptible nod of the President's head, the Chaplain raised his voice in prayer. He prayed in accents that were so gentle and so persuasive, they must have turned the hardest heart to blessed thoughts of peace and love and fraternity and union. And then again all eyes were fixed with intense strain upon the face of the President.

"Gentlemen of the House of Representatives, this measure upon which you are now deliberating..."

With a sudden blow that startled every living soul within its hearing, the Speaker's gavel fell.

"The President," said he with a superb dignity that called down from the galleries a burst of deafening applause, "must not make reference to pending legislation. The Constitution guarantees him the right 'from time to time to give to the Congress information of the Union.' He must keep himself strictly within the lines of this Constitutional limit, or withdraw from the bar of the House."

A deadly pallor overspread the face of the Chief Magistrate till it seemed he must sink then and there into that sleep which knows no awakening, but he gasped, he leaned forward, he raised his hand again imploringly, and as he did so, the bells of the city began to toll the hour of midnight.

The New Year, the New Century was born, but with the last stroke, a fearful and thunderous discharge as of a thousand monster pieces of artillery, shook the Capitol to its very foundations, making the stoutest hearts stand still, and blanching cheeks that had never known the coward color. The dome of the Capitol had been destroyed by dynamite.

In a few moments, when it was seen that the Chamber had suffered no harm, the leader of the House moved the final passage of the Act. The President was led away, and the Republican Senators and Representatives passed slowly out of the disfigured Capitol, while the tellers prepared to take the vote of the House. The bells were ringing a glad welcome to the New Century, but a solemn tolling would have been a fitter thing, for the Republic of Washington was no more. It had died so peacefully, that the world could not believe the tidings of its passing away.

As the dawn broke cold and gray, and its first dim light fell upon that shattered dome, glorious even in its ruins, a single human eye, filled with a gleam of devilish joy, looked up at it long and steadily, and then its owner was caught up and lost in the surging mass of humanity that held the Capitol girt round and round.

THE END